THE DEVELOPMENT

BOOKS BY JOHN BARTH

THE FLOATING OPERA

THE END OF THE ROAD

THE SOT-WEED FACTOR

GILES GOAT-BOY

LOST IN THE FUNHOUSE: FICTION FOR PRINT, TAPE, LIVE VOICE

CHIMERA

LETTERS

SABBATICAL: A ROMANCE

THE FRIDAY BOOK: ESSAYS AND OTHER NONFICTION

THE TIDEWATER TALES: A NOVEL

THE LAST VOYAGE OF SOMEBODY THE SAILOR

ONCE UPON A TIME: A FLOATING OPERA

FURTHER FRIDAYS: ESSAYS, LECTURES, AND OTHER NONFICTION, 1984–1994

ON WITH THE STORY

COMING SOON!!!

THE BOOK OF TEN NIGHTS AND A NIGHT: ELEVEN STORIES

WHERE THREE ROADS MEET

THE DEVELOPMENT: NINE STORIES